Corn
An American Indian Gift

Written by Gare Thompson

Contents

Corn Long Ago

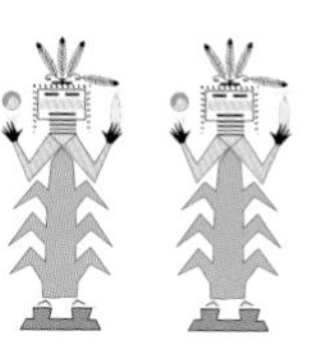

How did corn first begin to grow? Some American Indian legends from long ago try to explain it.

One legend tells about three sisters named Corn, Beans, and Squash. Corn was the oldest sister. She had yellow hair and was very tall. Everywhere she walked, corn plants grew in her footprints.

No one knows for sure how corn first began to grow. But it has been grown for thousands of years. The oldest corncob fossil was found in Mexico. It is about 7,000 years old!

The American Indians who lived in Mexico learned to plant corn and help it grow. Often it was the only food they had to eat. They called it **maize**. This means "bread of life."

Long ago people in Mexico ate corn.

American Indians grew corn for food.

American Indians learned to use all the parts of the corn plant. They used the leaves to make baskets, beds, and shoes. They even used the **stalks** to make roofs for homes. Soon items made from the corn plant were used as money to trade.

Then the Pilgrims came to North America. American Indians shared corn with them. They taught the Pilgrims how to plant and grow corn. They showed them that it could be used many ways.

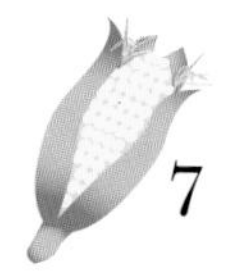

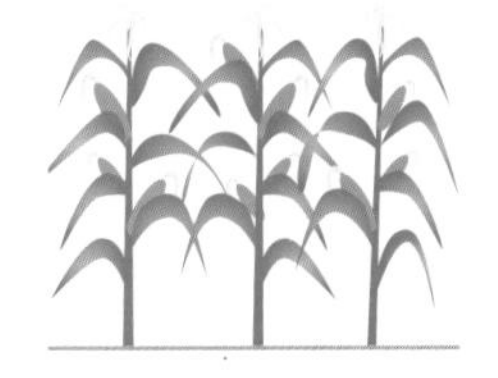

An Important Crop

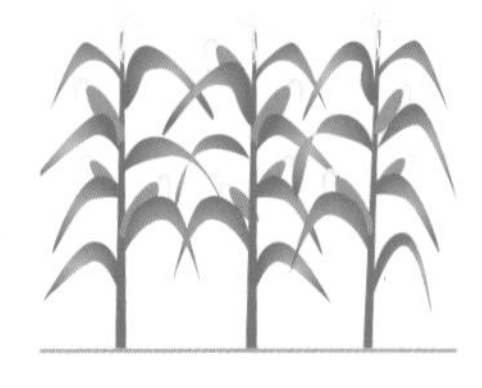

Today farmers all around the world grow corn. It can grow in both warm and cold places. Corn is an important **crop** in North America, China, France, Russia, and India.

More corn is grown in the United States than in any other country. The area where it is grown is called the Corn Belt.

Many farmers in China grow corn.

A young corn plant grows in a field.

Corn takes about four to six months to grow. It is usually planted in the spring. After a seed is planted, it takes about two months for the plant to grow into a strong cornstalk.

Soon buds appear on each stalk. These buds take about two months to become fully grown **ears** of corn. Then the ears are ready to be pulled off the stalk.

Some corn is left on the stalk a month after it is ripe. It dries out and turns brown. Then the dry, hard corn can be used as food for animals. Farmers use this corn to feed cattle, hogs, chickens, and sheep.

Corn is a good food for animals.

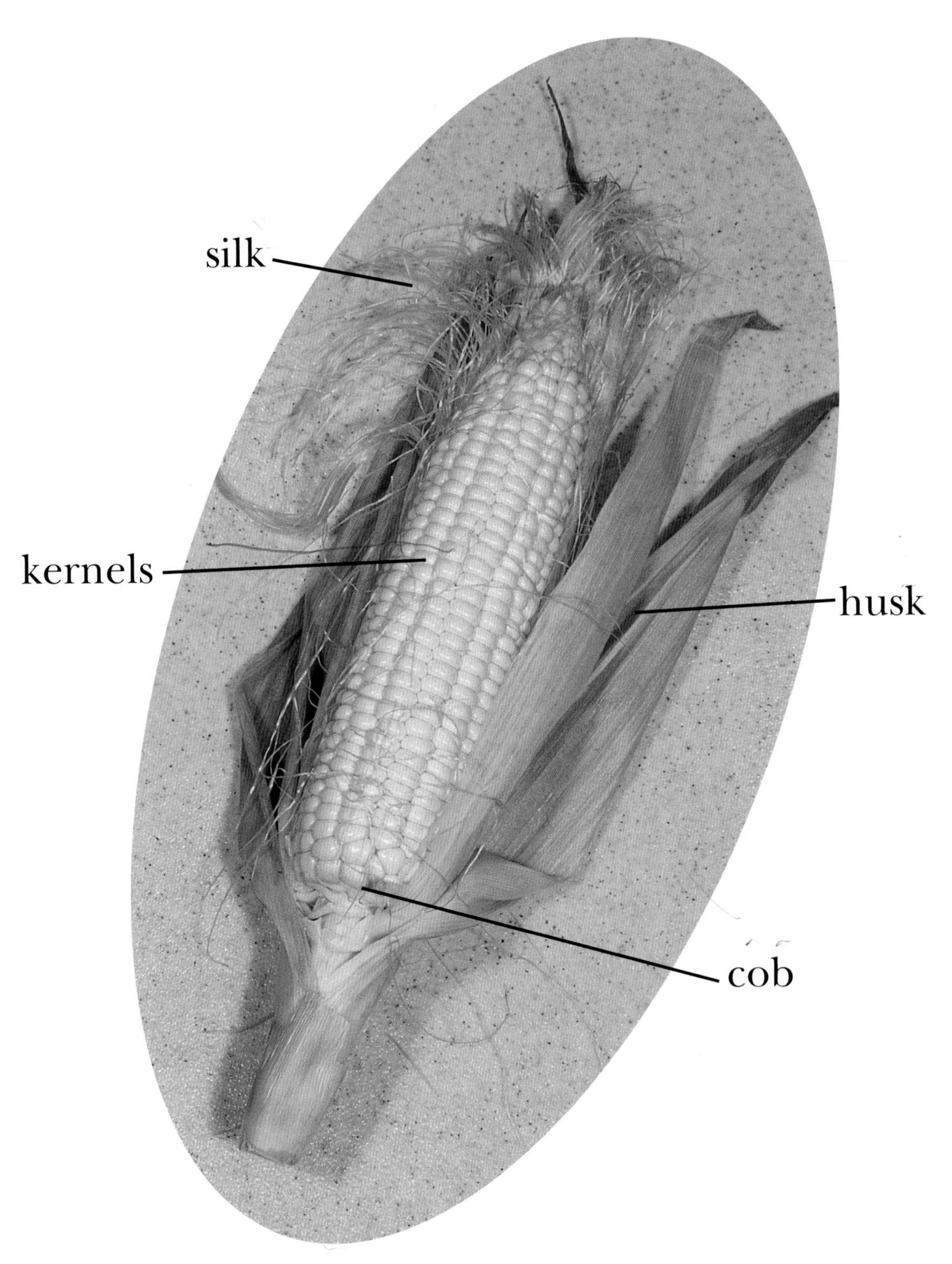

The corn plant has many parts.

The core of an ear of corn is the **cob**. It holds rows of corn **kernels**. They are the small parts on the cob. They look like teeth. Some kernels are soft, and others are hard. Kernels can be blue, black, white, orange, red, or yellow.

Corn **husks** are the tough leaves that grow around an ear of corn. They protect the kernels from insects and bad weather. Corn **silk** grows inside the husks with the kernels. Silk is soft and stringy.

A Tasty Food

There are many different kinds of corn. The two kinds people like to eat are sweet corn and popcorn.

Sweet corn has soft and sweet kernels. When the corn is ripe, the ears are picked from the stalk. The kernels are taken off the cob. They can be frozen or packed in a can.

Sweet corn can also be eaten from the cob. The ears of corn can be boiled or roasted. This is called eating "corn on the cob."

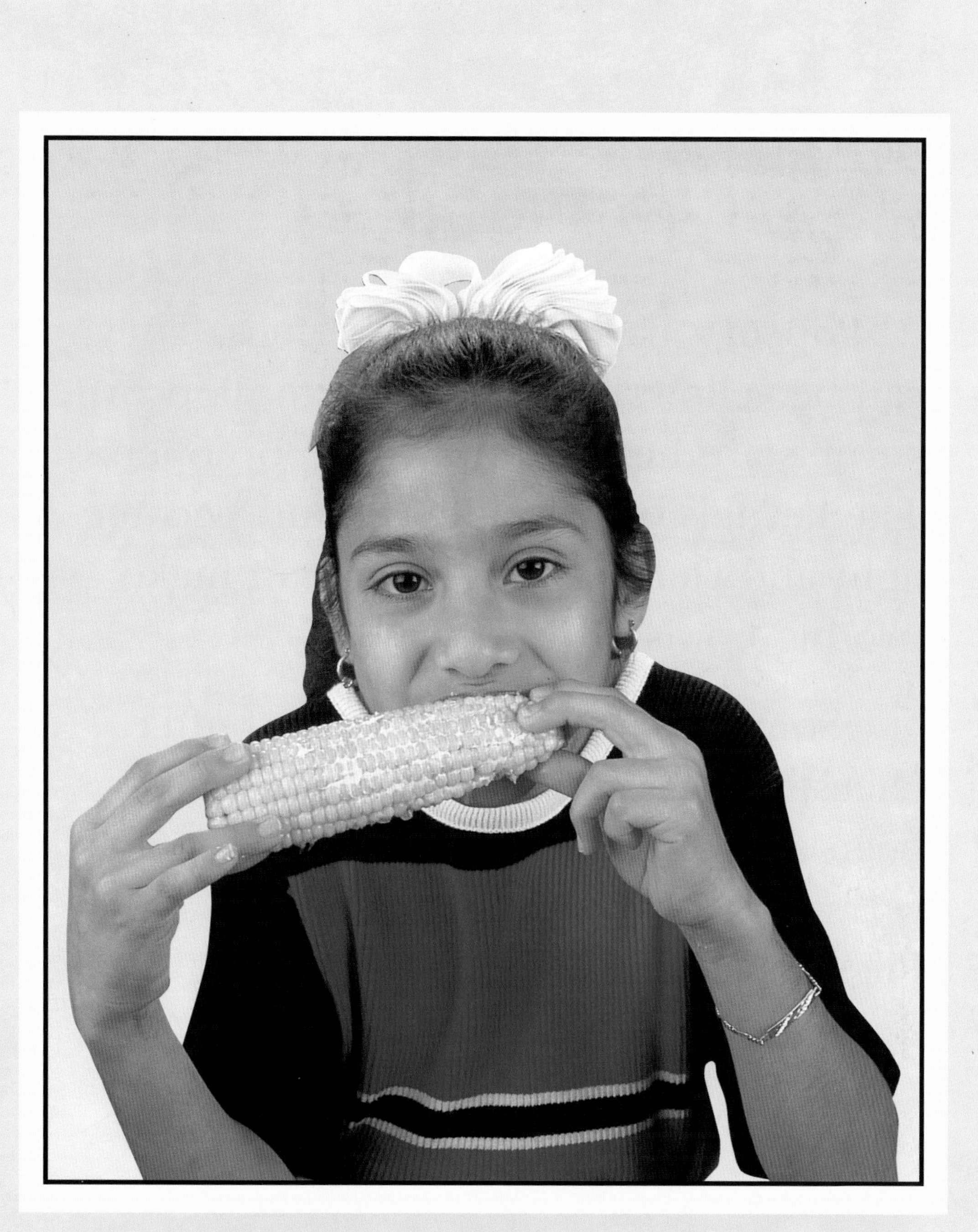

Corn on the cob is a tasty food.

Popcorn has very hard kernels. They can be yellow, orange, or white. Popcorn kernels are heated until they pop open. The kernels turn inside out and become light and fluffy. A single ear can make two big bowls of popcorn!

Sometimes people add salt, butter, cheese, or caramel to popcorn. It has been a popular snack for hundreds of years. Long ago American Indians and Pilgrims ate it!

Popcorn is a popular snack.

Whole kernels are not the only way corn can be eaten. Dried ears of corn can be ground into **cornmeal**. This can be used to make cornbread, tamales, grits, corndogs, and cereal. People of all ages enjoy foods made from cornmeal. Many children like to eat corndogs at the fair.

Tamales are a Mexican food made from cornmeal.

More Than Food

Corn is not only used as food. It is sometimes used to make medicine, paper, paints, plastics, and soap. It has even been used to build a palace!

Corn is a plant that we can eat, make things from, and feed to animals. No wonder it is called the bread of life.

Corn was used to build a palace in South Dakota.

Glossary

cob core of an ear of corn

cornmeal ground corn kernels

crop vegetables or fruits that are grown

ears parts of the corn plant that hold the corncob and kernels

husks leaves that grow around an ear of corn

kernels seeds of a corn plant

maize another name for corn

silk part of an ear of corn that is soft and stringy

stalks stems of the corn plant